The Letters of Mariya Iris

I Love Mariya Iris, Volume 1

Antonio Carlos Pinto

Published by Antonio Carlos Pinto, 2023.

THE LETTERS OF MARIYA IRIS

First edition. November 23, 2023.

Copyright © 2023 Antonio Carlos Pinto.

ISBN: 979-8223187745

Written by Antonio Carlos Pinto.

THE LETTERS OF
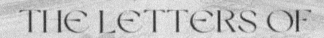
MARIYA IRIS

Dedication

I dedicate this story to all the brave hearts who dare to love, even in the face of the uncertainties of destiny. May they find in the pages of this journey an echo of their own experiences, and that, in the end, they can smile with the certainty that love is the guiding star that lights our path, even in the darkest nights. Let each page be a reminder that in the end, the heart always finds its home.

Thanks

Thank you to every kind soul who allowed this story to come to life. To those who inspired with their love and courage, who were the light amidst the shadows and who showed that, even over the longest distances, hearts can beat in unison.

I am grateful to the friends and family who have supported this journey with their constant warmth and encouragement. You were the foundations on which this story was built.

To the tireless team who made it possible to share this narrative with the world, my deepest gratitude. Each effort and dedication were like careful brushstrokes on a collective work of art.

And last but not least, to the readers who embark on this journey, who open their hearts to Antony, Mariya and their stories, my most sincere thanks. May these pages bring a little light and warmth to your own paths.

With gratitude,
Antonio Carlos Pinto.

Title

A h, in the ephemeral dance of life, who can count the stars in the sky or the sands by the sea? Who can measure the pulse of emotions, the rhythm of love?

Tears, like pearls, adorn the face of time, and smiles like sunbeams perfume the garden of existence. And in our footsteps, we sometimes leave indelible marks on the hearts of others, like stones thrown into a lake, generating ripples that reverberate into eternity.

But in the mantle of destiny, we are not mere toys. We are intrepid navigators, captains of our own saga. In each choice, in each hug, we weave the intricate embroidery of our journey.

And in the end, when twilight pours over the horizon, it is in the honesty of the heart that we find the true compass. For in the tangle of loves and dislikes, it is the flame of genuine love that illuminates our path, and the seed of forgiveness that cherishes our souls.

Introduction

At the far reaches of time and space, where the limits of love stretch beyond sight, a story emerges that echoes through the ages. It is a narrative of intertwined souls, of destinies intertwined by invisible threads, where love knows no borders. This is the saga of Antony, a young man whose heart was shaped by the seasons of love, and whose journey took him across continents and hearts.

After the end of a relationship he believed to be eternal, Antony embarks on a quest to find the true meaning of love. On this path, he comes across women who leave indelible marks on his soul: Angela, the flame that goes out; Christina, the postponed reunion; Yslena, the temporary departure; and Mariya Iris, the promise of the future.

*Uniting these chapters of your life are virtual letters, which transcend time and space, carrying confidences, dreams and secrets. Through them, Antony and Mariya Iris find themselves in a digital ether, where words come to life and dance to the sound of their hearts.

This is an odyssey that reminds us that, even in a world of physical distances, the heart is capable of finding its home in another. Join us on this journey, and allow yourself to believe that, in the end, love always finds its way.

Preface

In the winding web of destiny, Antony found himself immersed in a whirlwind of emotions, where love and disappointment danced a dance of shadows. His first kiss with Angela, in the rain, was a storm of passion that drew sighs from his lips and echoed in the recesses of his soul, but time, mercilessly, sealed their fate with their cruel separation.

Thus, loneliness became his most faithful companion, and tears, his confidants. Angela's shadow hung over his heart, an echo of a love that crumbled like dust in the wind. Each night was a pilgrimage through the dark corridors of longing, where sighs mixed with the empty echo of his own heart.

And then, like a ray of light in the midst of darkness, came Christina, with her compassionate, comforting love. Her kiss was the balm that healed the wounds of Antony's soul, a promise of renewal and a glimpse of a future full of hope. But the plot of destiny is capricious, and separation was, once again, the price to pay.

The third chapter of this odyssey was written by Yslena, whose motherly love warmed Antony's heart. His kiss was the promise of a safe home, a haven in the midst of the storm. But it was also a farewell, a necessary departure for José's growth, the fruit of a love that could not be.

And then, like a silver thread that transcends time and space, Mariya Iris emerged, bringing with her a connection that defied the boundaries of the physical world. His kiss, although virtual, was a flame that burned with intensity, a link that united hearts separated by geography.

Thus, Antony found himself entangled in a tangle of loves and disappointments, each kiss a page in the epic of his heart. Fate, that relentless weaver, wove a tapestry of emotions, where love and loss danced in an eternal contradance.

What choice is left for a heart divided between loves that have deeply marked it? Such is the tragedy of intertwined affections, a journey of tears and laughter, of dreams and goodbyes, where each step reverberates in the soul for all eternity.

Prologue

A t the core of each soul lies a sanctuary where the lines of destiny and continents intertwine. It is a recess where love is a silver thread, weaving its plot through the digital ether, taking flight until it finds rest in the distant eyes and heart, thousands of leagues away.

This is the saga of Antony and Mariya Iris, whose destinies intertwine in the vast virtual waters. Their souls waltz to the rhythm of digital words, exchanging secrets and desires that cross the barriers of space and time.

However, love is not a mere word, but a flame that demands more. It requires bravery to face the specters of the past, resilience to overcome the barriers of the present, and faith to believe in a future where hands touch no longer through screens, but skin to skin.

Antony, in his navigation through lost and rediscovered seas of love, realizes that the real warmth of the heart is not replicated, and that passion is a force that burns beyond the reach of time and space.

This is an epic of love that transcends logic, an odyssey that reminds us that, even in a world of physical distances, the heart is capable of finding its home in another. Follow us on this journey, and allow yourself to believe that, in the end, love always follows its own destiny.

Chapter 1: Unusual encounter

On the night of the intoxicating beginning, when music and relaxation danced in the air, my friends and I gathered to witness a rock performance in the local square. It was one of those nights that promised to be memorable, full of energy and permeated by promises of indelible experiences.

It was then that I caught a glimpse of Angela for the first time. An overwhelming presence, his dark hair dancing in the wind, and those eyes that seemed to contain the very essence of the night. Beside him, Angelica and Jessica, his sisters, each emitted their own aura of fascination.

We approach, enveloped by the vibrant cadence of the music, driven by the promise of new friendships. Laughter and dialogue filled the air, forging instant complicity. Angela had the gift of lighting up a room with her smile, and I, undeniably, succumbed to her charm.

- Greetings, my name is Antony.

- Nice to meet you, Antony. I'm Angela.

Time seemed to expand as we talked. The words flowed as if we already knew each other from other lives, and the connection between us was tangible. As the night progressed and stars dotted the sky, we found ourselves alone on the shore of a lake, enveloped by the serenity of the night.

And then the rain broke out, as if the universe itself longed to be a witness to the magical moment about to happen. Without hesitation, we ran in search of shelter under a tree, but fate had another outcome in store. We were soaked, shivering from the cold, but none of us seemed to care. Under the leaden blanket of rain, our eyes met.

- Angela, you look resplendent.

- Antony, I feel so good by your side.

And the kiss that followed was the promise of a love that would transcend any obstacle.

The rain enveloped us, creating a magical and passionate scene. Our gazes intertwined, hearts beating in rhythm, and the world around us seemed to disappear, leaving just the two of us there, immersed in the dance of raindrops.

At that moment, the kiss became the promise of a love that would overcome any barrier. It was the seal of a beginning, the harbinger of a journey that none of us would have dared to predict that night.

In the days that followed, Angela and I grew even closer. Our conversations became poetry, words that caressed the soul and laid bare shared dreams. The hours seemed to fly by when we were together, and each goodbye was the guarantee of a new meeting.

The visit to Angela's house represented a step further in the journey we were on together. My presence, so different from Angela's family's Catholic environment, caused surprise, but did not prevent warm acceptance. Angela's parents noticed the sincerity in my eyes and the way I cared for their daughter.

- Father, mother, we would like to ask for your permission to date.

- Are you sure about this, Angela? You have known each other for a short time.

- Yes, I love Antony. Please let us date.

So, in a rush of pure courage, I asked to date Angela in front of her parents and herself. My heart was beating strong, but determination drove me. Angela looked back at me, a smile that lit up the room, and her parents, after a brief pause, nodded. The love between us was palpable and that was what truly mattered.

And so, that night, destiny intertwined our destinies, launching us on a journey of discoveries and emotions that would alter the course of our lives forever.

Chapter 2: The Second Encounter

At the second meeting with Angela's family, a transcendent milestone in our journey, I arrived punctually, determined to make a lasting impression. Angela was at my side, radiant and confident.

As I crossed the threshold of the house, I was overcome by a profusion of feelings. It was like entering an unexplored universe, full of symbolism and rites that were foreign to me. The walls adorned with sacred images and the subtle aroma of incense created an atmosphere that mixed warmth and solemnity.

Angela's parents, the honorable Mr. and the gracious Mrs. Santos, they welcomed me with warm smiles, and with gentle solicitude they sent me away. As time progressed, the initial tension gave way to affable dialogue and shared laughter.

I admired the skill with which Angela transmuted between these two worlds, paying homage to traditions and celebrating the uniqueness of each one. It was a fine balance, but she made it simple.

During the banquet, I shared stories and experiences with Angela's parents, listening with interest about the faith that was so charitable to them, and sharing a little of my own spiritual journey. Despite the dissonances, I perceived an understanding that exceeded words.

The meal gave way to a night of music and conversations around the table. I noticed how harmony reigned in that corner, and how love and respect were the pillars that built that family.

- It was a pleasure having you with us, Antony. We look forward to your visit on other occasions.

- Thank you for the generous welcome. It meant a lot to me.

Upon leaving that home, a deep gratitude permeated my being. Angela accompanied me to the threshold, and before saying goodbye she wrapped me in a hug that conveyed trust and affection.

As I made my way home, I knew that this second meeting was more than just an introduction. It represented an imposing step in building a bridge between our universes, a testimony that true love is capable of transcending all dissimilarities.

From that moment on, Angela's life and mine seemed to take on a new depth. Each day stood as an invitation to explore the limits of love and understanding.

The days intertwined into weeks, and the weeks into months. We shared not only laughter and stories, but also dreams and desires. Each encounter turned into a learning opportunity, a chance to explore the subtleties of our intertwined souls.

However, physical distance sometimes cast its shadow over the horizon. I was sorely missed, but Angela's epistles, handwritten and filled with affection, were balms for my heart.

Our world was a delicate melody between two realities, two cultures that merged in a surprising way. Each challenge we faced, each moment of overcoming, strengthened the foundations of the love we built together.

And then, in a rush of courage and authenticity, I asked Angela to be my girlfriend in front of her parents. Angela's loving gaze and her parents' warm acceptance sealed the commitment. I felt a mixture of gratitude and resolution in my chest. I was ready to face the challenges that life still had in store for us.

Our journey had just begun, and the future stretched out before us like a blank canvas, ready to be colored with the paints of love.

Chapter 3: Bonds that grow stronger

After a few meetings with Angela's family, I had a new confidence in our bond. The way she introduced me into her universe, with reverence and affection, attested to the depth of the feelings that blossomed between us.

The days flew by like birds in flight, and every moment with Angela was a gift. Together, we explored the hidden corners of the city, uncovering hiding places and forging memories that would be engraved in our hearts for all eternity.

Our rapport was tangible, as if we were made for each other. In the interludes of silence, our souls intertwined in a language that did not lack words. It was a connection that transcended the limits of time and space, a bond that grew stronger every day.

Angela also felt gratitude for having me in her life. I gave her a new perspective on the world, injecting her with a dose of audacity and adventurous spirit that she had never known before. We joined forces to face challenges and celebrate victories, weaving a future full of promises.

Angela's letters remained like rays of sunshine on cloudy days. Each hand-drawn word carried with it the aroma of his presence, the warmth of his love. As time passed, these missives metamorphosed into treasures, jealously guarded in my heart.

However, physical distance still hovered like a shadow over the horizon. We missed each other, and the desire to be together grew every day. However, we were fully aware that the love we shared was more powerful than any obstacle.

- Angela, my dear, although we only met recently, I feel in the depths of my soul the desire to spend the rest of my days by your side. Will you agree to marry me?

- Antony, my beloved, nothing would bring me more happiness. Yes, I accept to join you in marriage!

And then, under the glare of a starlit night, I understood that it was time to move forward. With a heart full of bravery and steadfastness, I asked for Angela's hand in marriage in the presence of her parents and her. Angela's loving gaze and her parents' warm acceptance were confirmation that we were on the right path.

And so, at that precise moment, the future unfolded before us like a blank parchment, waiting to be filled with the colors of love and shared life.

Chapter 4: The challenge of distance

As the months passed, Angela's trajectory and mine began to follow new paths. Daily obligations weighed on our shoulders, demanding that we divide our time between work and studies.

Angela, with eyes full of firmness, dove headfirst into the treaties, hoping to build a solid future. Each page turned represented a step closer to his desires, but it also meant less time by my side.

In turn, I took on the responsibility of looking after my grandmother. A role that I played with tenderness and devotion, but that also required my dedication and energy. The days became a frenetic dance between my duties and the desire to be by Angela's side.

The physical distance between us became a perennial presence, a shadow that hovered in moments of solitude. The meetings, once frequent and full of laughter, became rare, being confined to the final days of the week.

- I miss you, my love. How is everything there?
- Challenging, but the idea of the two of us gives me strength to move forward.

However, despite the distance, the love we had for each other continued to pulse vigorously in our hearts. Each moment shared became even more precious, as if the cosmos were conspiring to strengthen the bonds that intertwined us.

We learned to value the quality of the moments we spent together, finding inventive ways to keep the flame burning. Epistles and messages became bridges that spanned the distance, transporting words of love and longing from one heart to another.

So, even when faced with the challenges that life imposed on us, Angela and I faced the distance with resolution and hope. Because we were aware that, in the end, the love we shared was more powerful than any obstacle.

Chapter 5: The Shadow of the Past

As time flowed, the distance between Angela and I became an incessant battle. Daily obligations seemed to pull us in opposite directions, creating a gap that was difficult to bridge.

Meanwhile, Bruno, Angela's ex-boyfriend, reappeared in her life. With wealthier resources and a past that was already known to Angela's family, he seemed to offer a solution to the challenges that distance imposed on us.

Angela's family, attentive to their daughter's well-being, began to suggest the possibility of a reconciliation. The pressure was tangible, and Angela found herself torn between the past and the present, between the security that Bruno promised and the deep love she felt for me.

I, in turn, sensed the presence of a shadow in our relationship. The unspoken words hung in the air, creating a tension I didn't know how to dispel. I felt the urgency to find a way to overcome the challenges that life imposed on us.

At each of our encounters, Bruno seemed to be present in some way, a silent presence that hovered over us. Angela struggled to reconcile the feelings that tormented her, while I struggled to keep the flame of love that united us alive.

- Angela, is everything okay? I feel like there's something wrong between us.

- I'm confused, Antony. The family pressures and Bruno reappears. Forgive me.

And so, in this whirlwind of emotions, Angela and I found ourselves at a crossroads. The path ahead was uncertain, and each choice had the power to shape the direction of our lives.

While the future remained shrouded in mystery, one thing was certain: the love we had for each other was true and strong enough to face any challenge. Now, it was up to us to find the strength and courage to follow the path that our hearts showed us.

The days turned into a whirlwind of emotions for Angela. Bruno's presence evoked long-dormant memories and feelings, triggering an internal battle that she could no longer ignore. The family, concerned about his well-being, saw in Bruno a solution to the challenges that the distance imposed by our relationship presented.

Angela found herself torn between what her reason and her heart told her. On the one hand, Bruno represented stability and familiarity. On the other hand, I was the love that made her feel alive, the laughter that filled her days and the hope for a future full of possibilities.

Meanwhile, I felt the tension growing between us. Bruno's shadow loomed over our relationship, a constant presence that made me question the fate of our love story with Angela. I knew I needed to find a way to dispel that shadow, to prove to Angela that together we could overcome any obstacle.

The conversation Angela and I needed to have was inevitable. It was time to share our fears, hopes and uncertainties. Sitting under the soft starlight, we opened our hearts to each other, revealing our deepest truths.

Angela admitted the internal struggle she was facing. Bruno represented a known past, a security that tempted her to go back on her choices. However, she also confessed that the love she felt for me was what made her feel alive, and that life with me was a path she longed to follow.

I, in turn, expressed my determination to face the challenges that life imposed on us. I understood Angela's family's concerns, but I was willing to fight for our love. It reminded her how strong we were together, how much we could overcome any obstacle.

That night, under the twinkling stars, Angela and I committed to facing together whatever fate had in store for us. The shadow of the past was still present, but now we knew we could face it hand in hand, ready to write the next chapter of our love story.

Chapter 6: The Journey and the Confrontation

Angela's family, distressed by the dilemma that involved her, came up with a plan to help her make a decision. Under the pretext of visiting a distant aunt in another city, they hatched the plot.

Secretly, they decided to take Bruno with them, keeping him hidden until the opportune moment. Angela left, without suspecting anything, and I stayed behind, my heart eaten away by doubts and the feeling that something was about to change.

While Angela found herself immersed in a new city, Bruno took the opportunity to get closer to her. With sweet words and gestures that evoked memories of a time that seemed to be behind him, he courted her. Angela felt torn, enveloped by a whirlwind of conflicting emotions.

Meanwhile, I anxiously awaited news from Angela. The weeks seemed to drag by, each day an endless wait. Uncertainty hung in the air, and I knew something had changed.

When Angela returned, the tension was palpable. Our reunion was full of expectations and apprehension. She knew the time had come to confront the feelings that haunted her.

That night, under the starry sky that had witnessed so many moments of our journey, Angela and I opened up completely to each other. The words were spoken, the fears and insecurities exposed. Angela confessed Bruno's persistent presence in her life and the conflicting feelings it caused.

With a heavy heart, I listened to every word, absorbing the complexity of the situation. I understood Angela's struggle, but I also knew that our love was strong enough to overcome any challenge.

In that moment of truth and vulnerability, Angela and I faced the crossroads that fate presented us with. It was time to decide the future of our love story, to choose whether we would give what we had built together a chance or whether we would go our separate ways.

The moment for confrontation had arrived, and Angela knew she needed to be honest with me. Under the starry sky that seemed to hold her breath, she opened her heart.

Angela confessed that, although she spent two weeks with Bruno, she didn't cheat on me. However, he admitted that his feelings for Bruno were far from just memories. A part of her still loved him, a love from the past that was resurfacing with strength.

My gaze showed a mixture of understanding and pain. I understood the complexity of Angela's feelings, but the news still hit like a blow. The love we shared was strong, but now it was facing a challenge that neither of us had anticipated.

With a heavy heart, I made a difficult decision. I needed time to reflect, to understand what those revelations meant for our future. I asked Angela for a break, a moment away so we could both sort out our own feelings.

That night, we said goodbye in heavy silence. The stars witnessed the anguish that hung over us. Each step away from each other felt like an echo of the uncertainty that permeated the air.

As Angela returned to her home, her heart heavy with uncertainty, she knew the future of our love story was hanging in the balance. The words spoken that night echoed in her mind, and she felt the weight of the choices she would have to make.

Meanwhile, I sought a space of stillness to digest everything that had been said. The stars shone above, like silent guardians of our hearts.

Chapter 7: New Paths

I stepped away to find clarity amidst the whirlwind of emotions surrounding me. I needed time to reflect on what was truly important in my life, and silence was the ally that would allow me to do that.

Meanwhile, in the context of work and studies, I entered a new phase of my life. The busy time provided a welcome distraction, a way to channel my energy and focus.

The computing course became a journey of discovery and learning. Among the unfamiliar faces, I found one presence that stood out. Christina. His bright eyes and captivating smile were like a light in the crowd.

The connection between us was instantaneous, a spark of energy that brought us together in an almost magical way. Christina, with her passion for technology and her agile mind, found a worthy intellectual partner in me.

The time we spent together in classes and on course projects became precious to both of us. With each meeting, the admiration we felt for each other grew, and the friendship transformed into something deeper.

- Antony, I see that something has been worrying you lately. Want to talk about it?

- I don't think I'm ready yet, Christina. My apologies.

However, as Christina's feelings deepened, she realized that I was experiencing a time of transition in my personal life. She could feel the shadow of an unfinished story hanging over me.

While Christina and I shared laughter and challenges, my heart still belonged to Angela. I knew I needed to face this truth, and that the choices I made from then on would have a lasting impact on my life.

And so, I found myself at a crossroads, with two paths before me. Angela's love and the new passion that Christina represented. Each choice would have its price, and I knew the future was uncertain.

Chapter 8: Search for Answers

Days passed and I made a difficult decision. To protect Christina's heart and preserve my own feelings, I decided to withdraw from the computer course. It was the only way I could see to avoid the pain of a situation that seemed increasingly complex.

Meanwhile, Christina felt my absence palpably. Uncertainty and worry consumed her, and she knew she needed to find answers. Determined, she began a search for my whereabouts.

With determination, she went after my friends, asking delicate and persistent questions. One by one, they were reluctant to divulge information, until finally, it reached Joe.

Joe, my friend and confidant, couldn't hide the worry in his eyes. He knew how difficult a time I was going through and he understood my decision to walk away. With a heavy sigh, he ended up revealing my address.

Christina wasted no time. Driven by concern and the desire to understand what was happening, she headed to my house. Every step was a mix of nervousness and determination.

When she got there, she knocked on the door with her heart racing. The moment was full of expectations and uncertainties, but she knew she needed to face the situation...

When she knocked on the door, Senhora Paulina, my grandmother, was the one who welcomed her. His gentle, experienced eyes watched her curiously, recognizing her as someone who was important to me.

Christina, with a lump in her throat, asked for me. Lady Paulina sighed, noticing the anguish in her eyes. She understood the depth of my suffering.

With a tenderness that only years of wisdom can provide, Senhora Paulina explained that, although I didn't share all the details, she knew that my heart was in pieces because of Angela, my ex-girlfriend.

Senhora Paulina's words were like an echo of what Christina already suspected. She felt the connection between me and Angela, a story that seemed far from having an end.

Upon hearing those words, Christina felt a mixture of compassion and sadness. She knew I was fighting an internal battle and that my heart was torn between two women I loved in different ways.

Determined to offer me her support, Christina thanked Mistress Paulina and set out in search of me, determined to face whatever she found.

Upon entering my house, his steps were cautious. She knew the moment was delicate and that every word would be important. As she approached my room, she could feel her heart pounding in her chest, prepared for whatever she found inside.

Christina entered my room with a heavy heart. The room seemed infused with the energy of difficult decisions and conflicting emotions.

When I saw her standing there at my door, I was momentarily speechless. Our eyes met, carrying with them all the complexity of the moment.

Christina didn't wait for me to speak first. With the sincerity that characterized her, she began to speak. He expressed his concern, his desire to understand me, and his unconditional support, regardless of the choices I made.

Her words were like a balm to me. They brought comfort and the feeling that I was not alone on my journey. I opened my heart, sharing the pain I felt over Angela's distance and the confusion that situation brought.

Together, we faced the truth and vulnerability that conversation demanded. The silence that followed was filled with mutual understanding and the certainty that we were willing to support each other, regardless of the path we chose.

As the hours passed, Christina and I discovered that despite the complex circumstances, there was a genuine connection between us. A friendship that transcended the barriers of my broken heart.

At the end of that night, I felt a thread of hope intertwining with the uncertainties that still persisted. I knew the road ahead wouldn't be easy but now I was no longer alone.

Chapter 9: The Moment of Surrender

With grandmother leaving for her sister's house, the house was suddenly silent. It was as if the space was charged with a new, palpable energy, an opportunity for Christina and me to confront what was between us.

Christina, sensing the change in the environment, knew this was the moment we had both been waiting for. Alone in my house, we looked at each other with a mixture of nervousness and desire, aware that we were about to give ourselves over to this love that had been growing between us.

Words were unnecessary at that moment. The silence was filled with the soft sound of our hearts beating in unison. Every touch, every look, carried with it the promise of a deeper connection.

Christina and I slowly approached, as if the world around us disappeared. The heat of our bodies merged, creating a synergy that transcended words.

And then, at the height of that surrender, we came together in a passionate kiss. It was a moment that sealed the love we had discovered for each other, a confirmation that we were willing to face challenges together.

In the heat of that moment, we allowed ourselves to be vulnerable, setting aside the doubts and uncertainties that haunted us. The love we shared was real and palpable, and in that moment, that was all that mattered.

While the world outside took its course, Christina and I surrendered to the present, building a new page in our stories.

Time passed and Christina and I continued to live the love we had discovered for each other. Our relationship was intense and full of precious moments, but without the labels and commitments that could complicate things.

Until one day, Christina gathered the courage to make a revelation that would change the course of our lives. With eyes full of emotion, she announced:

- Antony, I'm pregnant.

The news echoed in the air, creating a silence filled with surprise and expectation. For a moment, I felt the world spin around me. The idea of becoming a father was both terrifying and incredibly exciting.

Our eyes met, seeking comfort and support in that moment of revelation. We knew we were facing a new crossroads in our lives, one that would force us to make difficult decisions and face the consequences of our choices.

As the news settled in our hearts, Christina and I hugged, feeling the strength of that moment. We were about to embark on a journey that would change our lives forever, a journey that would bring us together in an even deeper way.

And so, faced with the unexpected revelation, Christina and I found ourselves facing a new reality. Together, we would have to find a way building a future that now included not only the love between us, but also the love for a small being who was about to enter our lives.

Chapter 10: The Heart's Dilemma

As Christina and I faced the news of our pregnancy, fate seemed to have prepared a surprising turn of events. The phone rang, interrupting the charged silence of the moment.

I answered, and on the other end of the line, Angela's familiar voice echoed in the room. She was back, willing to rekindle what we once shared.

The dilemma that now presented itself was painful and complex. My heart was torn between two women, each representing a different chapter of my life.

Angela, with our past and the memories we shared, represented a love story that still echoed in my heart. And now, with the pregnancy announcement, Christina and I were about to start a new chapter together.

Angela's words were filled with emotion, with a genuine desire to start over. She was willing to face challenges and fight for what she believed to be true.

As I listened, the storm of emotions within me seemed to gain strength. I knew I was faced with a choice that would change the course of our lives.

The silence that followed was almost tangible, a pause in time where all possibilities seemed suspended in the air.

My heart was pounding as I faced the difficult conversation with Angela. The words I needed to say were like weights on my shoulders, but I knew it was time to be honest.

With determination, I arranged one last meeting with Angela to tell her the truth. We met under the tree where I kissed her for the first time and told her about the new person in my life, about the unexpected pregnancy and about the complexities that were now part of my world.

Angela listened silently, each word hitting like an arrow, bringing a mix of emotions. She understood the gravity of the situation and the reality that was now before us.

I explained that getting back together with her at that time was not viable. I would be a father and have new responsibilities and commitments. Plus, I admitted that I still hadn't completely gotten over Angela's time with Bruno.

That conversation was an end to the story we shared. It was a moment of farewell, of closing an important chapter in our lives.

Tears fell, hearts sank, but we both knew it was the right decision. We hugged, sharing one last moment of intimacy and goodbye.

As Angela left, I stood there, watching her go. The silence was heavy, but there was also a sense of relief, a feeling that we could finally move forward, each on our own path.

Chapter 11: Mistrust

I returned from the conversation with Angela with a heavy heart, but also with a feeling of relief at having finally put an end to that story. I reached out to Christina to share the news, hoping that together we could face the next chapter of our lives.

Upon hearing my words, Christina fell silent for a moment, her gaze fixed on the floor. A shadow of doubt crossed her eyes, and she finally looked at me with a serious expression.

- Are you sure about this, Antony? - she asked, her voice full of suspicion. - Because I have a feeling you're still seeing Angela.

Christina's words hit me like a punch in the gut. I couldn't believe that the woman I loved didn't trust me. I tried to explain, swearing that the conversation with Angela had been definitive, but my words seemed to fall on deaf ears.

The trust we had built was crumbling before our eyes, replaced by a cloud of uncertainty and distrust. I felt helpless, unable to prove my honesty in the face of Christina's suspicions.

And so, an abyss formed between us, separating us emotionally. We were both caught in a whirlwind of emotions, not knowing how to overcome this crisis of confidence that threatened the love we shared.

As night fell upon us, Christina and I faced the most difficult challenge we had ever encountered: rebuilding broken trust and finding a way to move forward together.

The room was filled with the tension that hovered between us. The words of distrust echoed in the air, creating an invisible barrier between us.

I looked into Christina's eyes, desperate to make her understand the sincerity of my words. I swore once again that my conversation with Angela had been final, that I had closed that chapter of my life.

However, the words seemed to fall on deaf ears. Christina was trapped in her own insecurities and fears, unable to accept the truth in the face of the suspicions that tormented her.

The distance between us seemed to grow by the second, and I felt a mixture of frustration and sadness. I loved Christina and I never imagined a moment like this could come between us.

On the other hand, Christina felt trapped in a whirlwind of conflicting emotions. She wanted to believe me, but the shadows of distrust seemed to persist.

The night wore on, but the silence between us was deafening. Each was faced with a dilemma: how to rebuild the broken trust and find a way to move forward together?

The fate of Christina and I was now in the hands of our own decisions and our ability to overcome the obstacles that life threw at us.

Chapter 12: Time for Reflection

The tension between Christina and me was palpable, and we both felt the need for space to breathe and reflect on the direction of our lives.

With an emotionally charged hug, Christina announced her decision to spend a few weeks at her mother's house. It was a time to distance yourself, to gain clarity about your feelings and the path you wanted to take.

Although reluctant to see Christina go, I understood the importance of this time for both of us. I knew that the arrival of a child brought with it responsibilities and decisions that would impact our lives in a profound way.

As Christina prepared for her trip, I hugged her tenderly, promising her support and understanding, no matter what she decided.

And so, Christina left, leaving me behind in a silence filled with meaning. The house, once full of laughter and love, was now silent, reflecting the introspection everyone was facing.

For me, those days of solitude became a journey of self-knowledge and reflection. I found myself confronted with the choices I had made and the future that now lay before me.

Meanwhile, Christina allowed herself time to connect with her own emotions and longings. She knew she needed to find the answer to the question that echoed in her mind: what did she really want for her future?

And so, physically separated, Christina and I embarked on a journey of personal discovery, each aware that our choices would shape not only our own lives, but also the life of the child about to be born.

Weeks passed, and the silence in my house was almost deafening. I spent my days reflecting on the choices I had made and the future unfolding before me.

When the moment finally arrived, and Christina returned from her mother's house, the atmosphere was filled with anticipation and apprehension. Our eyes met, searching for signs of clarity and determination.

It was then that Christina announced her decision with a serenity that hid the pain she was feeling. She wouldn't come back to me. His choice was to remain at his mother's house for good.

The impact of his words was like a blow to my chest. I found myself faced with the reality that the future I had imagined was unraveling before me.

With tears in my eyes, I hugged Christina, knowing that moment represented a goodbye. We separated with one last look full of emotion, aware that we were following separate paths.

After Christina left, my house felt like an even deeper void. I found myself alone, surrounded by memories of a love that now belonged to the past.

It was in this moment of solitude and reflection that I made a decision that would shape my future. I decided that, for now, I would no longer get emotionally involved with women. It was a time to focus on myself, my parenting journey, and finding my own path.

And so, I faced the future with a mixture of determination and resignation. I knew there were challenges ahead, but I was willing to face them with courage and an open heart for what destiny had in store.

Chapter 13: A New Beginning

I looked around the empty house, memories of happy days now seemed distant and melancholy hung in the air. It was time to make a decision that would change the course of my life.

With determination, I decided that it was time to seek a new beginning, far from the memories that haunted me. I decided to go live with my sister in the countryside, where the calm of country life could help me heal the wounds that time had not yet healed.

When I announced my decision, Christian, my sister, welcomed me with open arms. She knew how much I had suffered and was determined to help me find the peace I so deserved.

Together, we packed our bags and embarked on a journey towards a new chapter of our lives. The countryside landscape stretched out before us, promising to be the setting for new beginning full of possibilities.

I allowed myself to absorb the serenity of the environment, the sound of the birds and the gentle breeze that caressed my face. It was as if nature was whispering words of comfort and renewal.

In the days that followed, I began to reconnect with myself. I immersed myself in activities that brought me closer to the simplicity of country life, finding solace in the peaceful routine and warm support of my sister.

As the months passed, I began to feel the weight of suffering give way to a new sense of hope. With each dawn, I saw the promise of a future that, although uncertain, brought with it the possibility of new beginnings and redemption...

Chapter 14: The Return

Ten years had passed since I left the city in search of a fresh start in the countryside. Now, an urgent call brought me back.

My grandmother, the person who had always supported and loved me unconditionally, was facing a difficult time in her life. I felt a responsibility to be by her side, to return the love and care she had always received.

Upon returning to the city, I came across a familiar scene, but at the same time, strangely different. The streets that had once witnessed my happiest moments now seemed to carry an aura of nostalgia and longing.

Arriving at my grandmother's house, I was greeted by warm hugs and emotional looks. I felt grateful to be there, to have the opportunity to be by her side at such a delicate moment.

In the following days, I dedicated myself entirely to caring for my grandmother. I listened to her tell stories from the past, laughed with her at funny memories and, sometimes, simply stayed by her side in silence, sharing the weight of that moment.

While caring for my grandmother, I also had the chance to meet familiar faces and longtime friends. Each meeting was an opportunity to relive memories and, in a way, remember who I was before I left.

My presence in the city brought with it a sense of reunion and reconnection. Even in the face of the sadness that surrounded my grandmother's situation, I felt the human warmth and love that permeated every moment.

And so, I was back in the city I once left behind. With a heart full of gratitude and a deep sense of belonging, I faced the challenges that awaited me, knowing that, in the end, love and family ties were the true foundation of my life.

As the days went by, I immersed myself more and more in the routine of caring for my grandmother. Every moment with her was precious, and I strived to make that time as comforting as possible.

My grandmother, despite her physical fragility, demonstrated a strength of spirit that inspired me. He told stories from his youth, shared life lessons and, above all, conveyed an unconditional love that spanned the years.

In moments of pause, I explored the city that saw me grow up. Every corner brought with it a memory, a glimpse of the past that now blended with the present. I met childhood friends, relived adventures and, little by little, I felt part of that place again.

The news of my return spread throughout the city, and people came to greet me with warm smiles and words of welcome. It was as if the community was celebrating the return of a prodigal son.

In the evening, I would often sit next to my grandmother, looking out the window and watching the sunset. It was a moment of silence, of deep connection with the feelings that permeated my heart.

The days turned into weeks, and I knew goodbye was near. My grandmother, despite her physical weakness, emanated a serenity that reassured me. She was ready to face the next stage of her journey, and I was determined to support her through this process.

While the city continued to welcome me with open arms, I felt grateful to have had the opportunity to return. Those days had taught me the importance of family, community and love that transcends time.

And so, I prepared myself for the moment when I would have to say goodbye to the city once again. But this time, I carried with me not just memories, but also a deep understanding of what really matters in life.

Chapter 15: The reunion

The news of my return to the city spread like wildfire, reaching the attentive ears of Yslena, Christina's younger sister. Upon learning that I was back, she decided to prepare a surprise to mark this reunion.

This is how Yslena brought with her a precious thing: José, my son a 10-year-old young man who carried in his features the mixture of his origins and the promise of a future full of possibilities.

The meeting between father and son was full of emotion. I looked into José's face, seeing in him a part of myself that had been distant for a decade. And, at the same time, I noticed my grandmother's influence and love in the way José expressed himself and smiled.

The joy that emanated from José was contagious, and my heart was filled with gratitude for having the opportunity to know him and be part of his life. It was a new beginning, a chance to build a relationship that even with lost time, promised to be meaningful and special.

Over the next few days, José and I spent time together, exploring the city and sharing stories from our lives. Every moment was an opportunity to get to know each other better, to build bonds that transcended blood.

Yslena, watching the reunion between father and nephew, felt her heart overflow with joy. She knew how much it meant to José and me and she was happy to have been part of this surprise that brought us together.

As the days progressed, José's presence brought new energy to my home. His laughter echoed through the halls, filling the spaces with the promise of a bright future.

And so, José, Yslena, I formed a bond that, despite the circumstances, was strong and meaningful. We were ready to face together whatever fate had in store.

Yslena's revelation about Christina getting married and traveling to Russia brought a mixture of surprise and understanding to me. I knew how unpredictable life could be, and the news that your sister had gotten married and decided to live abroad was a new chapter in our story.

The fact that Christina left José in Yslena's care until our reunion was a responsibility I accepted with an open heart. José's presence had become a blessing in my life, and I was determined to give my son the love and support he deserved.

Looking at José, I felt a mixture of gratitude and determination. I knew that situation brought with it challenges, but I was determined to be the best father I could be.

In the following days, José and I began to build a special relationship. We shared moments of learning, laughter and, above all, trust. I strived to be an example and support for José, knowing that every gesture and word was important in building this new chapter of our lives.

Christina's absence was felt, but the promise of a future reunion brought comfort and hope. I knew that, when that moment arrived, we would face the challenges together and celebrate the joys that life had in store for us.

As I looked into José's face, I saw in it not only the image of my own past, but also the promise of a future full of possibility and love. Together, father and son, we were ready to face whatever life threw at us.

And so, José, Yslena, I formed a new type of family, united by the strength of love and the determination to face together the challenges that life presented to us.

Chapter 16: New Horizons

Yslena's revelation brought with it a mix of emotions for me. I knew that the reunion between José and his mother, Christina, was eagerly awaited, but the news that they would possibly stay in Kiev, Russia, for a few years, messed with my expectations.

I looked at José, seeing a mixture of emotions in my son's eyes. Reuniting with Mom was a promise of love and reconnection, but it also meant leaving behind the home we had built together.

Yslena explained the reasons behind the decision. She wanted José to have the opportunity to spend time with his mother, to discover new places and cultures. It was a chance to expand horizons and create memories that would last forever.

I, although understanding Yslena's motives, felt a pang of sadness. I knew that José's departure would mean a temporary goodbye, but I was also aware that this was an important step in my son's journey.

In the following months, José and I prepared for the big trip. Every moment together was precious, and we made the most of the time we had.

The day of departure finally arrived, and the farewell was full of emotion. I hugged José tightly, promising that I would always be there for him, no matter the distance.

As I watched them leave, I felt a mixture of sadness and gratitude. I knew that this separation was temporary and that the reunion would be even more special.

And so, I faced a new chapter in my life, knowing that, despite the distance, the love that united me with José and my family would remain strong and unshakable.

Chapter 17: New Ties

Time had passed and life continued to weave its web of surprises and unexpected encounters. And Yslena found in Mariya Iris a friendship that transcended the limits of time and space.

The complicity between them was palpable, and together they faced the challenges and celebrated the achievements that university life brought. Mariya was the kind of friend who became an extension of her own family, and I knew I could count on her in any situation.

One day, while Mariya was looking through Yslena's clothes for something for a college event, Mariya came across a photo that piqued her curiosity. In the image, a smiling man, a young girl full of life and a radiant child formed a portrait of happiness.

Intrigued, Mariya asked about the man in the photo, and Yslena candidly shared the story of Antony, the former brother-in-law and father of her sister Christina's child. He spoke about the love between Antony and Christina, about the choices that life had led them to make and about the distance that now separated them.

The revelation brought a new dimension to the friendship between Yslena and Mariya. It was as if an invisible link united them, a connection that transcended the present and intertwined with the past.

Over the next few days, Yslena and Mariya shared their own stories and experiences. They laughed together, they cried together, and most of all, they supported each other every step of the way.

The discovery of the photo became a milestone in Yslena and Mariya's friendship, a reminder that life often surprises us with the bonds it creates between people.

And so, Yslena and Mariya continued their journeys, knowing that deep down, we were part of a complex web of stories and relationships that shaped who we were and who we were destined to be.

Mariya's interest in Antony was a silent seed that was beginning to sprout. She felt a special connection to the story Yslena had shared, and her curiosity about the man in the photo grew every day.

One afternoon, while Yslena and Mariya were in their dorms, Mariya finally gained courage and opened her heart to her friend. She confessed her feelings and growing curiosity about Antony.

Yslena listened to her carefully, understanding the delicacy of the situation. I knew that Antony's past was intertwined with his family's and that the introduction of a new person could bring challenges.

After the conversation, Mariya proposed something unusual: she asked Yslena to send an email to Antony, introducing her and sharing photos of them together at college. It was a way to break the distance barrier and, at the same time, a way to let Antony decide if he was open to a new connection.

Yslena, despite conflicting feelings, agreed to support her friend. She understood the importance of following her heart and was willing to help Mariya express her feelings.

In the email, they honestly described the friendship they shared, the special moments they lived together and their curiosity to meet Antony, the man who had played such a significant role in Yslena's life.

They attached photos smiling, celebrating life and the friendship that united them. It was a delicate invitation, a way of telling Antony that there was room in their hearts for new stories.

When sending the email, Yslena and Mariya eagerly awaited Antony's response, aware that, regardless of the outcome, they were taking a step towards the unknown.

Chapter 18: Reading the email

I was at the computer, looking at the screen with a mixture of curiosity and apprehension. The email from Yslena and Mariya had arrived, and I knew it could turn my life around.

With a deep breath, I opened the message. Yslena and Mariya's words flowed delicately, telling the story of their friendship, sharing moments of joy and celebrating the connection that brought them together. The photos captured genuine smiles and moments of complicity between them.

As I read each line, I felt a mix of emotions. I admired Mariya's courage in expressing her feelings and Yslena's sincerity in supporting her friend in this gesture.

It was an invitation to a new chapter, an opportunity to expand horizons and open your heart to new possibilities. I knew that that moment marked an important choice in my life.

After finishing reading, I remained silent for a moment, letting the words echo in my mind. I looked at the photo of them together, seeing the happiness on their faces.

Finally, with determination, I began to compose my answer. I shared my own words, expressing gratitude for Mariya and Yslena's sincerity, and talking about the importance of following your heart.

As I typed, I felt a new energy pulsing within me. It was as if that email was the beginning of a new chapter, a blank page ready to be filled with new stories and experiences.

When I finished the message, I clicked "Send" and felt a mix of nervousness and anticipation. He knew that the future was full of uncertainties, but he was willing to face them with an open heart.

And so, I waited, knowing that destiny had surprises in store and that I was ready to welcome them with open arms.

Chapter 19: An expected answer

Mariya was sitting in front of the computer, her heart pounding with anticipation. The email she and Yslena had sent to me represented a bold step, and now, the response was about to arrive.

When the new email notification flashed on the screen, Mariya felt a mixture of nervousness and joy. He clicked quickly, opening the message with his eyes shining with emotion.

The words I had written filled the screen, bringing a rush of warmth and comfort. I expressed gratitude for Mariya and Yslena's sincerity, and talked about the importance of following your heart.

Upon reading those words, Mariya felt a smile form on her rosy face. The answer I had given him was like a breath of fresh air, a confirmation that new possibilities were opening up before us.

With a sigh of relief and happiness, Mariya began typing her own response. He thanked me for my sincerity and expressed his joy at having the opportunity to get to know me better.

It was the beginning of a new stage, a blank chapter ready to be filled with new stories and experiences. Mariya was ready to face the future with an open heart.

When he finished the message, he clicked "Send" with determination and hope. I knew that the path ahead could be full of challenges, but I was willing to face them with courage and love.

And so, we waited..., with the certainty that destiny had something special in store for us.

I was in front of the computer, my heart full of anticipation. Mariya's response was awaited with a mixture of nervousness and expectation.

When Mariya's email arrived, I opened it carefully, reading every word carefully. His words were like a ray of sunshine, bringing warmth and joy to my heart.

Mariya expressed her gratitude and joy at having the opportunity to get to know me better. He shared his own heartfelt words, creating a bond between us that seemed to grow with each message.

I felt a special connection with Mariya. There was something comforting about the way she opened up and shared her feelings. It was as if the universe was conspiring to bring our paths together in a unique way.

Inspired by the moment, I decided to return the gesture. I selected a special photo, a memory of a happy moment that captured the essence of who I was.

Attaching the photo, I wrote a few simple words, expressing my gratitude for Mariya coming into my life. It was an exchange of moments, a way of building a bridge between us.

With a sigh of contentment, I clicked "Submit." I knew that gesture was more than just a photo. It was a step into the unknown, a promise that new horizons were about to open.

And so, I waited, knowing that the future was a blank book, ready to be filled with the pages of my own story.

Chapter 20: Waiting for an Answer

Days passed and I, with my heart full of expectation, anxiously awaited Mariya's response. Every free moment was filled with the hope that a new message would arrive.

However, time seemed to drag by while Mariya was on vacation at her parents' house. The peaceful and familiar setting surrounded her, making the days go by serenely.

I imagined Mariya, immersed in the warm atmosphere of her home, finding comfort in the presence of her family and childhood friends. The laughter and shared memories must have been making her feel renewed, but they also brought a certain delay in her response.

Meanwhile, I continued to look at my inbox, waiting for any sign of a new message. The silence was almost deafening, and uncertainty hung in the air.

I found myself imagining what Mariya was doing, how she was enjoying her vacation. Each moment of waiting was a mixture of anxiety and hope, a delicate dance between the promise of the future and the uncertainty of the present.

However, I knew that patience was a necessary virtue at this time. I understood that everyone deserved their time and space, and that Mariya's response would come when the time was right.

And so, I continued waiting, knowing that time was a powerful ally, capable of weaving destinies in surprising ways.

Chapter 21: New Memories

Finally, after a week of waiting, Mariya's response arrived. And I felt a mix of relief and joy when I saw the notification of a new email.

Upon opening the message, I was greeted by warm words and photo that captured moments of serenity and joy. Mariya shared her vacation at her parents' house, showing the park where she walked with he mother and the majestic horses on the farm.

The images were like windows to a distant world, bringing with them the peaceful and welcoming atmosphere of the place. Antony coul almost feel the gentle breeze and hear the sounds of nature.

Each photo was a new memory, a piece of the puzzle that made u Mariya's story. I felt like I was getting to know a more intimate side o her, a part of her life that made her even more special.

When I read Mariya's words, I realized how much she valued thos family moments. The connection between us seemed to grow with eac exchange, and I couldn't wait to find out what the future held.

With a smile on my lips, I began to prepare my own response. shared my appreciation for the photos and the stories they told. It was a if, through the computer screen, they were sharing a piece of their world

And so, the conversation between me and Mariya continuec weaving new memories and strengthening the bonds that united them.

Afterword

In the pages of this story, we witness the dance of love between continents and hearts, a dance that defies time and geography. Through Antony's words and emotions, we are reminded that love is an inextinguishable force, capable of transcending any obstacle.

Each chapter, each meeting and goodbye, leads us to reflect on the complexity and beauty of love. Angela, Christina, Yslena and Mariya Iris are more than characters; they are reflections of all the forms that love can take, of all the ways it can transform us.

This journey teaches us that love is not a straight line, but an intricate maze of emotions, choices and unexpected encounters. At each step, we are reminded that the heart is resilient, and that, even in the face of disappointment, it is capable of renewing itself.

May this story inspire us to believe in love's ability to surprise us, to take us beyond our own borders. May it remind us that, in the end, love always finds its way.

Epilogue

And so, time continues its eternal dance, weaving the destinies of Antony and Mariya Iris into a unique tapestry of experiences and memories. What began as a virtual exchange of words turned into a journey of love that transcended borders and defied time itself.

Angela, Christina, Yslena and Mariya Iris remain as stars that light up the sky of Antony's story, each leaving their indelible mark on his heart.

As the sun sets on the horizon, Antony and Mariya Iris find themselves at a new beginning, ready to face the challenges and joys that the future holds for them. And so, they walk together, knowing that in the end, true love never knows an end.

And so, the story continues...

Glossary

G **lossary:**

1. Digital Ether: The intangible space where virtual communications occur, transcending physical barriers and allowing connection between people in different parts of the world.

2. Geography of the Heart: The metaphor that describes how love can be influenced by geographic factors such as physical distance and location, but also how it is capable of transcending these barriers.

3. Internet Ocean: The poetic analogy that represents the vastness and depth of online interactions, where people can connect and share emotions, thoughts and experiences.

4. Dance of Souls: The poetic description of the exchange of words and emotions between Antony and Mariya Iris, representing the harmony and special connection they share.

5. Flame of the Heart: The metaphorical representation of true love, which burns deep within Antony's chest, defying time and distance.

6. Passion Beyond Reach: The idea that the passion between Antony and Mariya Iris is so intense that it goes beyond physical and geographical limitations, manifesting itself in ways that go beyond direct physical contact.

7. Tapestry of Experiences: The metaphor that describes the story of Antony and Mariya Iris as an intricate and beautifully woven fabric, formed by all the experiences, encounters and challenges they faced together.

8. The Persecuted: Term that denotes those who face challenges and adversities on their journeys, symbolizing struggle and resilience in the face of difficulties.

This glossary offers insight into the poetic and metaphorical terms used in the narrative, helping you understand the nuances and deeper meanings of Antony and Mariya Iris' story.

Don't miss out!

Visit the website below and you can sign up to receive emails whenever Antonio Carlos Pinto publishes a new book. There's no charge and no obligation.

https://books2read.com/r/B-A-RODAB-WLBRC

BOOKS 2 READ

Connecting independent readers to independent writers.

Did you love *The Letters of Mariya Iris*? Then you should read *Flight of Free Birds*[1] by Antonio Carlos Pinto!

"Flight of Free Birds - A Journey Through the Centuries of the History of Love and Passion.

This work brings together poetic tales and chronicles of lived and fictitious loves at different times, over the centuries. You will find narratives from the Middle Ages to the present, crossing historical periods and different social classes.

From the fiery romance of two lovers in a king's court in the 12th century, to the forbidden relationship between a princess and a commoner in the 18th century. And also the passionate love between a nun and a monk in the 20th century monastery and among other

---

romances. Each tale brings dilemmas, joys and pains that only true love can provoke.

Written by author Antonio Carlos Pinto, this work rescues the beauty of medieval poetry to sensitively describe intense human feelings. A prolific author, Antonio has already published three historical novels that immerse you in the atmosphere of the past.

Throughout its 100 pages, this book promises to take you on an exciting journey through the centuries, witnessing how this universal feeling called Love manifested itself in the most diverse eras and contexts around the world.

I hope you enjoy these stories that show how Love continues to transcend Time."

Read more at https://www.amazon.com.br/Antonio-Carlos-Pinto/e/B08ZYRK243/ref=aufs_dp_mata_mbl.

Also by Antonio Carlos Pinto

A Feiticeira de Shadowthorn
A Feiticeira de Shadowthorn
La Hechicera de Shadowthorn
A Feiticeira de Shadowthorn
The Witch of Shadowthorn - Heirs of Tomorrow

I Love Mariya Iris
The Letters of Mariya Iris

Império de Truvok
Realidades Alteradas
Altered Realities

Maya & Alex
Maya & Alex And the Mechanized Sun
Maya & Alex und The Mechanized Sun
Maya y Alex y el Sol Mecanizado

Seraphis
The Medium Seraphis and The Fifth Dimension
Der mittlere Seraphis und die fünfte Dimension

Stellar Exodus
Stellar Exodus and the Lost Dimension

The Sorceress of Shadowthorn
The Witch of Shadowthorn

Wastervale
Wastervale - Floresta Sombria
Wastervale – Der dunkle Wald
Wasttervalle - Bosque oscuro

Wastervalley
Waster Valley - The Dark Forest

Standalone
Maya & Alex: E o Sol Mecanizado
O Médium Seráfis e A Quinta Dimensão
Revoar Dos Pássaros Livres
Flight of Free Birds

Êxodo Estelar e A Dimensão Perdida
Teoria da Viagem no Tempo através da Confluência da Relatividade e
Astrofísica
As Cartas de Mariya Iris
María Espoleta

Watch for more at https://www.amazon.com.br/
Antonio-Carlos-Pinto/e/B08ZYRK243/ref=aufs_dp_mata_mbl.

About the Author

Antonio Carlos Pinto é um escritor apaixonado pelo ofício de cria histórias de ficção científica e fantasia. Sua vocação para a escrita surgiu j na infância e se consolidou ao longo dos anos por meio de muito estud e dedicação à escrita.

Especializado em livros de ficção científica, fantasia e romance épicos de aventura, Antonio tem uma habilidade singular par transportar os leitores para outros mundos, sejam eles reais o imaginários. Entre seus livros mais conhecidos estão A Feiticeira d Shadowthorn, Wastervale e Todos os Amores.

Sua escrita fluida e envolvente remete tanto a tempos antigos quant a cenários futuristas. Antonio domina a língua portuguesa e sua nuances, o que lhe permite elaborar tramas complexas e textos ricos er detalhes.

Além de livros para o público adulto, Antonio também escreve ficçã peculiar para os jovens leitores. Suas histórias cativantes incentivam gosto pela leitura entre adolescentes.

Com sua imaginação fértil e seu talento primoroso para a narrativa, Antonio Carlos Pinto segue firme em seu propósito de levar ao público obras instigantes, que divertem e emocionam seus leitores.

Read more at https://www.amazon.com.br/Antonio-Carlos-Pinto/e/B08ZYRK243/ref=aufs_dp_mata_mbl.

About the Publisher

Antonio Carlos Pinto é um escritor dotado de uma mente criativa que sempre esteve imersa no poder das palavras. Sua incursão na arte da escrita teve início na infância, quando sua paixão por contar histórias começou a ganhar forma. À medida que os anos passaram, dedicou-se incansavelmente a aprimorar suas habilidades literárias.

Ele deseja compartilhar um pouco sobre seu estilo de escrita, que considera singular e inovador. Em suas obras, busca infundir vida nos personagens e nas narrativas através de uma abordagem que denomina "Sombroespério".

Esse estilo não se limita a uma única categoria, permitindo-lhe explorar ficção científica e dark fantasia, romance e poesia, assim como temas relacionados à religiosidade e espiritualidade.

A raiz do "Sombroespério" não repousa apenas na imaginação, mas sim na fusão de diversos estilos literários. Anteriormente, suas narrativas amalgamavam elementos dos estilos Gótico, Romântico, Modernista

Pós-Modernista, dando origem ao que ele denominava "Neo-Romantismo Sombrio".

Esse estilo almejava combinar a intensidade emocional do Romantismo com a atmosfera sombria e elementos sobrenaturais do Gótico. Ademais, incorporava técnicas de narrativa fragmentada e a exploração da subjetividade do Modernismo, juntamente com elementos metaficcionais e a desconstrução narrativa do Pós-Modernismo.

A inserção de convenções tradicionais shakespearianas culminou na gênese do "Sombroespério". Essa sinergia entre o Neo-Romantismo Sombrio e o estilo característico de Shakespeare resulta em uma expressão literária ímpar e inovadora.

"Sombroespério" espelha a profundidade emocional do Neo-Romantismo Sombrio e a eloquência dramática de Shakespeare, criando uma abordagem que desafia e comove o leitor.

Antonio Carlos Pinto espera que essa breve introdução ao seu estilo de escrita tenha sido esclarecedora e aguarda ansiosamente para compartilhar mais sobre suas obras e explorar as possibilidades de colaboração.

Read more at https://www.amazon.com.br/Antonio-Carlos-Pinto/e/B08ZYRK243%3Fref=dbs_a_mng_rwt_scns_share.

Milton Keynes UK
Ingram Content Group UK Ltd.
UKHW012027301123
433552UK00001B/92